For Florence B. Freedman

EZRA JACK KEATS

Louie

AGES 3-5

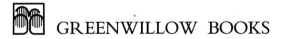

GREENWILLOW BOOKS

A DIVISION OF WILLIAM MORROW & COMPANY, INC. · NEW YORK

Library of Congress Cataloging in Publication Data   Keats, Ezra Jack.   Louie.   5.81
I. Title.   PZ7.K2253Lo   [E]   75–6766   ISBN 0-688-80002-5   ISBN 0-688-84002-7 lib. bdg.

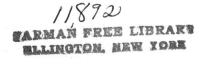

Susie and Roberto were putting on a puppet show.
They had spent a lot of time making the puppets.
Kids were trying to find seats next to their friends.
"Wow! Everybody's here!" said Susie.

"There's Louie," said Roberto.
"I never heard a word out of him."
"Me neither," said Susie.
"Well, let's get started."

The curtain opened.
A mouse puppet appeared on the stage.

The mouse introduced Gussie.
When Louie saw Gussie, he stood up.
"Hey, sit down!"
"We can't see through you, Louie!"
"C'mon, sit down, will ya?"
Louie just stood and stared.

"Hello!" he said.

"HELLO!   HELLO!"

"What's going on?" asked Susie.

Roberto peeked over the stage.

"It's Louie!" he whispered.

"He's talking to Gussie. He won't stop.

What'll we do?"

Susie thought for a moment.

"We'd better have Gussie answer him."

"Hi, Louie," Susie said in Gussie's voice. "Nice to see you.
But me and the mouse gotta get on with the show.
Will you please sit down? There's lots more to come."
Louie sat down. The place got quiet
and the play continued. The kids
laughed at the adventures of
Gussie and the mouse.

When the show ended, the puppets bowed.
Everybody cheered and clapped.
Louie jumped up and clapped loudest and longest.

As everyone was leaving, Susie and Roberto saw Louie.

"Would you like to say good-bye to Gussie?" Susie asked.

Louie grabbed the puppet and held on to it.

"What'll I do now?" Susie whispered to Roberto.

"Gussie is very tired," explained Roberto.

"She has to go home now."

Louie waited a minute, then let go of Gussie.

Susie and Roberto started off.

Louie waved until they were out of sight.

Then he walked home.

He went into his room
and sat on the floor.

He dreamed he was feeding Gussie
from a huge ice-cream cone.

Suddenly Gussie disappeared! And the cone, too!

Louie was falling

down

down

down

Now he was floating.
There were kids all around.
They were making fun of him.
"Hello, hello!"
"Nah—it's good-bye, good-bye!"
"Oh, yeah—hello and good-bye, Louie!"

"Louie," his mother called.

"Louie," she called, "what are you doing?"
He didn't answer. He was still sad from his dream.
His mother went on, "Someone slipped a note
for you under the door. It says,

'Hello! Hello! Hello!
Go outside and follow
the long green string.'"

Louie got up and went outside.